Savior / Destroyer

An Esar-Haden Tale

H. Rad Bethlen

Rooster & Raven

For the Daughters of Zeus and Mnemosyne

Author Statement Concerning Artificial Intelligence

The way I write consist of several phases.

1. Idea generation.
2. Research.
3. Story development.
4. Outlining.
5. Writing the rough draft.
6. Editing and rewriting.
7. Editing and polishing.
8. Copy editing.

I will *occasionally* use AI during the research phase if I can't locate some bit of information on my own—but I try to locate it on my own first.

I will *occasionally* use AI during the story's development if I get stuck on something—but I try to resolve my own story issues first.

I *intentionally* use AI during the copy editing phase as a stand-in for a copy editor, which I can't afford to pay for yet which I don't want to go without.

A copy editor is the last set of eyes to look at a manuscript to check for grammar, usage, spelling, and punctuation mistakes. I ask the AI copy editor to make suggestions on corrections. I evaluate those suggestions. If I agree, I make the changes.

I don't use AI for anything else.

Be comforted that this story was written by a human being for other human beings.

H. Rad Bethlen

Esar-Haden leaned with his back against the wood paneling of the library wall—waiting as patiently as any dark elf could—as the wizard flipped through the pages of a book.

Diffuse light filtered through twin windows at the end of the room. A chandelier hung above the table, flickering magical orbs of light in place of candles. Magical effects greeted him at every turn. Doors opened and closed without being touched. Feather dusters darted, leaving quick-fading sparkles in their wake. Even dirty dishes marched themselves to the kitchen, spilling not a crumb.

Esar-Haden, on being directed through the mansion by a man-servant in impressive livery, saw no other servants. "Do the linens launder themselves?" he asked his guide. He received no answer.

In the next chamber four women practiced a choral piece. Their harmony drew Esar-Haden's attention away from the annoyed searching of the wizard, a surface elf, who, with a word of magic, yanked free a massive tome from a nearby shelf. The book flew to a halt above the table then floated to a rest before the wizard, opening as it did so.

"Oltropp," the elven wizard glanced from the book to the dark elf, his long, light brown hair framing his diamond-shaped face, "that despicable halfling," he looked back down at the open pages before him, "says you're the best." His tone indicated disbelief or accusation, Esar-Haden couldn't tell which. In the adjoining room the women stopped their song and began to converse on the finer points of their craft.

"Sisters?" enquired Esar-Haden, indicating the women with a point of his thumb at the closed door. The elven wizard looked up from his book.

"Mother and sisters," he said. "Your employer, head of the thieves' guild, Oltropp. You remember him, don't you?"

Esar-Haden could only imagine that when that clever halfling suggested a dark elf for the job, his client, a surface elf, bristled. Such a reaction would have amused Oltropp, who was chiefly concerned with entertaining himself.

Esar-Haden looked at the wizard. "Can you afford the best?"

"Humph! You must have crawled out of a profoundly deep gutter if you can't recognize fantastic wealth when you see it."

Esar-Haden pushed himself off the wall and strolled to the door. The women had begun the song anew and he wanted to hear it unmuffled by the wood, walls, and books. The door did not open. He sighed and without turning answered the elf. "The deepest, my sun-drenched cousin." He turned to face the wizard and smiled.

The wizard also smiled. "This amuses you, doesn't it? A rich and powerful surface elf, a wizard, no less, turning to a dark elf thug for help?"

"I'm easily amused." Esar-Haden walked to a plush chair across from the table and sat down. The wizard's face crinkled in annoyance. "The idea of a thieves' guild," continued Esar-Haden, "is a little silly, don't you think? If it weren't for the fact that we have to pool our gold to pay off government officials we would all be stabbing each other in the backs. It's the greater threat that preserves us."

The elven wizard frowned. "What was your name again?"

"Esar-Haden."

"Esar-Haden, I'm not concerned with the details of your profession, such as it is. I care about a scroll titled the

Chronicle of Mozer Qoth, a new acquisition at the Tower of Seven Gales."

Esar-Haden produced a thin throwing dagger from the interior of his left shirt sleeve and began to pick at his teeth. If he were lucky enough to meet any of the wizard's sisters he didn't want the remnants of lunch greeting them when he smiled. He wished the wizard had etiquette enough to offer him a glass of wine to swish around in his mouth. He glanced in the air about him, thinking that perhaps one floated nearby and he had failed to notice.

"Perhaps you aren't taking this seriously—"

"A smash and grab then?" interrupted Esar-Haden, turning back to the wizard.

"Smash and grab?" The wizard walked around the table and sat in the other upholstered chair. "My dear darkness dwelling *cousin.* In my time at the Tower of Seven Gales there were no fewer than," he held up four fingers, "break in attempts. One clever thief even attempted to pull down a section of wall with a golem he had somehow gotten control of."

Esar-Haden re-sleeved his dagger.

The elven wizard sat back, putting his fingertips together. "One thief was turned to stone. I believe he's still in the same spot, as a deterrent. Another was teleported to the Nine Hells. The golem-commanding thief was devoured by a swarm of fiendish centipedes. The golem?" He smiled. "Is gainfully employed. I can't recall what happened to the fourth but I can only assume they met with a horrible end."

"Soft entry, then?" concluded Esar-Haden.

"I can see by the look on your face that you're thoroughly confused." The wizard rose and returned to his books.

"I can do a soft entry," said Esar-Haden. "I'm the best, after all. It's just that I stick out due to the rarity of dark elves on the surface, also, my race is near-universally despised, so I'm not usually the go-to-guy for a confidence scam, seduction scam, or similar techniques."

The singing stopped. The wizard looked to the door. It swooshed open, revealing one of his sisters.

"Brother, you asked for me?"

Esar-Haden stood and turned to face the speaker.

Like her brother, her hair was long and light brown, blonde in places. She had well-shaped eyebrows over large pale green eyes that slanted at the corners. Her face tapered to a small chin, her nose was well shaped. A smattering of freckles gave her an air of child-like charm. She smiled demurely, revealing perfectly level teeth under well proportioned lips. She had white flowers woven into her hair. A pair of emerald earrings hung from her ears.

"My apologies. I didn't know you had a guest." She bowed and retreated from the room. As the door closed her eyes flashed, meeting Esar-Haden's, keeping them until the door broke the connection.

"Well mannered."

The wizard frowned. "I can only imagine the type of women that you're used to."

"Every type."

This brought a chuckle from the wizard. He stood and crossed his arms. The book he was reading closed itself. "I can't get into the details here. All I can tell you at this juncture is that you and I will gain entry to the Tower of Seven Gales. I will distract those who need distracting. You will sneak into the archives, deal with any obstacles, locate the *Chronicle*, and steal it. I will meet you later and we will conclude our transaction."

"Is that when I get devoured by fiendish centipedes?"

The wizard smirked. "If so, wouldn't Oltropp and the other thieves make it their lives' work to kill me?"

"It's the greater threat that preserves us."

"Are you up to it?"

"I'll have to gather a few things before we depart."

The wizard was pleased and went back to his books. Esar-Haden turned and began to leave but the wizard called after him. "I have to be sure." Esar turned. The surface elf looked him full in the face. "If murder becomes necessary—"

Esar-Haden laughed.

The wizard smiled, nodding his head. "Meet me in the back garden tomorrow at high noon. I know your kind love the sun. It will be amusing to watch you sweat and stumble around blindly."

Esar-Haden didn't feel the need to respond. He could find his own way out of the mansion. He assumed the right doors would open, the wrong ones stay shut. As he passed gaudy statues and overly-lacquered woodwork he wondered what the wizard had meant by, "obstacles."

· · ·

The garden was a quilt of yellow, orange, and pink pastels, criss-crossed with ribbons of rose-colored stepping stones. The air shimmered with a rainbow of reflected color. The mingled scents of the flowers radiated out—a welcoming invitation. Esar-Haden arrived at the garden earlier than the appointed time. She surprised him when she spoke.

"You must not be used to such displays." Her hair was done up in elaborate braids. Her pale green eyes regarded him. She wore a simple muslin blouse and workman's trousers. She held a pair of sheers in her delicate fingers. The flesh of her bare arms was pale and as flawless as the petals of her well-tended flowers.

"Such beauty is rare." He meant her beauty, of course, and she caught his meaning, smiling in response.

He couldn't help but smile in return. He scanned the garden. "Your work?"

"All of us," she answered. "My mother and sisters, that is. My brother is far too busy, although," she looked to a corner of the garden. "He does grow some things he needs for spells."

"Your father?"

She looked from the flowers to the man who stood dangerously close to her (he was a dark elf, after all, and armed, his twin daggers hanging from his belt), shielding his eyes. "In the capital."

"I see," said Esar-Haden. "A wizard, like your brother?"

She looked at him, studying him, with such innocent curiosity it made him blush, not something he often did. "Yes."

"In the caves I grew up in, there were no flowers like these," he said. "The surface above was rock and sand. Although there was the occasional desert rose."

"A cave?" She tilted her head. "I couldn't imagine it. How gray and drab."

"Oh?" said Esar-Haden. "Nature took her time sculpting the caves, and she hid subtle beauty within. There are massive stalagmites, which the imagination shapes into fantastic brutes. There are cathedrals of soda straws. Pools of water so clear and still you would never know they were present, unless you broke their surface. In the desert sky above, the stars wrap around you, embracing you in their eternal mystery." He worried he was laying it on a bit thick but he had gotten carried away.

As Esar-Haden spoke she studied him. "You're not at all what I imagined."

"Ever meet a dark elf?"

"No," she said, "I'm afraid of them."

"You should be."

"Should I be afraid of you?"

"Certainly," he said, "but not today. Today I'm in awe of your garden," he looked at her, "and of your beauty." A few moments of silence passed as Esar-Haden admired the garden and the gardener.

She watched him with unabashed curiosity. "My brother told me about you."

Esar-Haden looked at her. "Oh? What does your brother know about me?"

"He says that it's rare for a dark elf to leave the darkness below. He says that makes you—different."

Esar-Haden shrugged his shoulders. "I suppose."

"He says that you're more virtuous than you pretend."

Esar-Haden couldn't help but chuckle.

"My brother says that you were born with a bright soul. He says you could have been an artist or a poet. But the culture you grew up in would have tried to kill that part of you. He wonders if those elements are hidden away, waiting for someone to make you feel safe, so that part of you can return."

Esar-Haden watched her as she spoke. She had a strange look in her eyes, as if she was already infatuated with the idealized, romantic figure she was defining. 'Why the hell is he feeding her all this non-sense?' He wondered. 'She was probably pestering him about my presence. He had to tell her something. He wasn't going to tell her the truth.' He thought it best to play along. "If we can find time, I will recite some of my poetry for you." Not that he had any poetry.

She smiled. "I would enjoy that. I could put it to music, if you like."

Esar-Haden smiled.

A noise came from the house, interrupting them. It was the door. She turned and looked. "My brother."

"What's your name?" asked Esar-Haden, before she could run. She turned back to him with a skittish look on her face. No doubt she had never imagined giving her name, or wanting to give her name, to a dark elf.

"Esmé." She moved past him, making her way out of the garden.

Esar-Haden heard the wizard's boots click on the stone pathway. He turned to face his new employer. The sun was at its apex. He had to shield his eyes, which watered without mercy due to the sun's light.

"Fall in love?" asked the wizard. Esar-Haden didn't answer. "You scared her, poor child, she's sheltered, you know? She no doubt has an instinctual distrust of your kind."

"One would hope."

The wizard reached out and touched Esar-Haden's arm. "You look miserable, poor thing. Is it the sun?" He walked past Esar-Haden. "Ready?"

"How long is our journey? I forgot to ask."

The wizard had a good laugh at that. "Quaint." He paused to check the assorted spell component pouches about his person. "'Tis but a pleasant stroll in the sun, my tortured darkness dweller." He seemed satisfied with his cataloging and began walking. "Come."

The pair passed from the garden, heading down a gentle slope toward a large stand of oaks. The wild grasses grew to shoulder height. A cut path wove through the wilderness. At their approach small birds took flight.

"We'll teleport to a spot nearby," said the elven wizard. "Teleporting into the tower itself is impossible."

"Teleportation?" asked Esar-Haden. As he spoke, a glimpse of movement caught his eye. At first he took it for the grass yet it moved apart from that swaying motion. He watched out of the corners of his eyes, not wanting to give away that he had caught the movement. Her light brown hair mingled with the pale yellows of the grasses. Her off-white shirt provided just enough contrast to give her away. She was paralleling them.

The wizard looked over his shoulder at the dark elf. "Ever done it?"

Esar-Haden shook his head. "Still trying to figure out horses."

The wizard looked ahead. "You really are a fish out of water."

Esar-Haden ignored him. His eyes were on Esmé. She wove through the grass with ease, staying just out of her brother's peripheral vision. Esar-Haden looked at her, caught her attention, smiled, and winked. This drew a shy smile from her.

"You'll have to be patient," said the wizard, "while I scry to make sure we don't teleport into certain death."

"Seems reasonable," said Esar-Haden.

Esmé wasn't close enough to hear their words, not above the increasing breeze that now brought the loose strands of her hair into her face. She kept most of her attention on picking her footing, but she looked to Esar-Haden, afraid she would lose sight of him.

'She doesn't seem worried for her brother's safety, even with a dark elf at his back. She's curious about this exotic creature that's entered her sanctuary. What is this monstrous beetle on the delicate petals of your flower?'

He was not ignorant of the romance of it. He knew people were drawn to contrast. As the pair approached the forest the girl darted from the grass into the trees. Esar-Haden lost sight of her. 'I should have my wits about me,' he chastised himself. 'Not be fawning over some female.'

The grass gave way to a tight clumping of trees. The wizard snaked his way through them, trailing Esar-Haden behind him. Not far into the forest, the wizard came to a stop. Esar-Haden stepped up next to him. The wizard sat down with his legs crossed, closed his eyes, and began to meditate.

Esar-Haden heard her moving closer. He turned to see her break from the shifting light and shadow of the deep wood into the foreground. She caught his gaze and stopped. She darted behind a tree, taking partial cover from him. She stuck her head out and looked. He stepped closer, closing the gap.

Near the tree she hid behind stood a moss-covered obelisk. A large rough-cut emerald was embedded in the stone. It pulsed with a dull inner light. Esar-Haden scanned the area, spotting a second stone, then a third.

'I should have paid more attention to Soléne when she tried to teach me magic.' He laughed at himself. He hadn't thought about Soléne in some time. Memories of her were always bittersweet. 'Still, the few spells she taught me have made all the difference.'

Esmé stepped out from behind a tree. Esar-Haden looked at her. She clung to it for a moment, then stepped out in front of the tree, despite her insecurity. She reached up with one hand and pulled the strands of hair from her eyes. The emeralds in the stones pulsed. The light was echoed in the gems of her earrings, illuminating the slender curve of her neck.

Esar-Haden stepped toward her, saw her tense like a jackrabbit ready to take flight, and stopped his advance. 'Sure is a skittish thing,' he thought. He stepped back two steps, to where he had started. She smiled. 'She wants to come to me,' he thought, 'Or come almost to me, then have me pounce on her.'

Esar-Haden glanced over his shoulder at the wizard. He sat motionless, moving his lips without sound. Esar-Haden looked back to Esmé. She pulled away from the tree and stepped forward. She stood now on her own, not hiding or bracing herself against anything. The green glow of the emeralds fell on the pale skin of her forearms. Esar-Haden was captivated by her curious behavior. He watched and waited for her to either approach or disappear into the woods. Instead, she stood there, gazing at him.

"Esar?" The wizard spoke as if from a dream. At the sound of her brother's voice, Esmé crouched behind a thickly-leafed bush. Esar-Haden turned and looked at the wizard. "Esar?" repeated the wizard, reaching his hand out, searching for the dark elf.

"Here," said Esar-Haden, stepping up.

"Ready?" asked the wizard, his voice a whisper.

"Always."

The wizard began to chant, sparkles of magic falling from his fingertips as he drew a complex pattern in the air. His eyes opened but they were rolled back and the pupils could not be seen. Esar-Haden looked for Esmé. He saw her peering through the leaves of the bush. The thin streams of light cutting through the leaves began to twist and coil. The wizard's voice rose. Esmé leapt from the bushes, spinning away from the pair.

Everything went white.

. . .

The ground beneath Esar-Haden shifted, his feet sliding several inches before finding purchase. Dark shapes materialized as his vision returned. His hands went to his daggers. He was mollified when the looming shapes were revealed to belong to the pine trees surrounding him. Motion to his left caught his attention. The elven wizard was rising to his feet.

The pair stood in a small clearing. Pine trees hid everything else from view. The ground was a carpet of needles. At the sudden arrival of two new occupants in the grove a startled squirrel began to click its teeth. After a moment's protest it ran up the branch to cover.

"See, Esar-Haden, nothing to it." The wizard turned to face him. "Over there," he said, motioning with a limp finger, "although you can't see it, is the Tower of Seven Gales. Surrounding the tower is, of course, the town of Seven Gales." The wizard knocked the pine needles from his backside. "And inside the tower is the *Chronicle of Mozer Qoth*." He thought for a moment before continuing.

"The Tower is no grand palace. It's small and cramped. It was built by an eccentric old wizard named Seruli. He was more fond of books than people. So you can imagine what consideration he gave to living quarters. That's to our advantage. Most of the wizards who haunt the library during the day retire to their own homes in the town at night. There remains, however, a rotation of two wizards who live in the tower itself. They have the glorious job of keeping watch should anyone break in, or attempt it.

"It's not a bad position. I've held it myself. You get free run of the library. I happen to know who one of these two is, a man named Edward Heath. I know this because Edward and I have been enjoying a little romance through steamy letters written with a quickened pulse, if you catch my meaning."

"Ah, seduction," said Esar-Haden.

"That's right, and it's been playing out over a long enough timespan to be quite effective. Edward is salivating for me. He knows full well I'm unattainable. That makes it all the more tantalizing for him. He knows that I'm not allowed in the tower upon penalty of death. He knows that ours is a romance that can never be fulfilled. At least not until he leaves the tower."

"Or until you show up and declare that you can't wait," said Esar-Haden, "that you're willing to risk death to have him in your arms."

"Me in his," said the wizard, with nonchalance. "He will feel a masculine pride at having drawn me to him. He will feel the need to protect me from the dangers of being caught, from the injustice of my banishment. He will draw me in at once, as an act of principled rebellion."

"And to consummate—"

"That is none of your concern." Snapped the wizard.

"Ah, the seduction scam, always double-edged."

"All you know is a knife at an unprotected throat," said the elven wizard. "If you knew what the *Chronicle* was, if you had any idea what secrets are locked away, hidden in Mozer's mad scribbles, what it can do, what you could do with it," the elf laughed, "you would rent yourself out like the filthiest brothel whore just to get a glance at it."

Esar-Haden raised a skeptical eyebrow.

"Those fools have no idea," said the wizard, looking toward the Tower. The wizard stepped away from Esar-Haden. "I'll bring down the protective spells, open the door, and let you in. You know what to do from there."

"The second wizard?"

"That's your problem. Can you handle this or have I made a mistake?"

"Wizards are easy. As long as they don't see you coming, giving them time to catch you in their magic tricks, they're helpless."

The wizard smiled. "That kind of thinking will get you killed."

"When the scroll goes missing, won't you be found out?" asked Esar-Haden. "I mean, why would either of the two wizards take the fall if they don't have to? Won't they pin it on you?"

"Edward Heath comes from a rich and politically powerful family. His reputation and political ties are what gained him access to the tower, not his talent as a wizard. He has little of that. To even accuse him would cost the tower dearly. If they did accuse him there's no chance he would mention my name. Edward's sexuality is quite private. No, the fact that I had been at the tower will never come to light."

"Whomever this other wizard is, I feel sorry for him," said Esar-Haden, although he wasn't genuinely concerned for the fate of this second, unknown wizard. "Either I'll kill him," said Esar-Haden, "or he'll take the fall." He looked at the elven wizard. "Does your conscience bother you?"

The wizard smirked. "Come to the tower well after the sun has gone down, and the town is asleep. Keep hidden, oh, and," his smiled grew sinister, "watch out for the golem."

"Looks like I'm hanging out here for the rest of the day," said Esar-Haden, looking around at the pines.

"No, that won't do. What if someone else teleports in? They'll scry and spot you. You'll have to find somewhere in the countryside or in town to hide. You're a professional, should be easy. Maybe there's a local thieves' guild. You could make new friends." The wizard turned and started through the pines, giggling at his own joke. Although he disappeared from sight, his laugh lingered.

Esar-Haden sighed and began to take the same path as the wizard when he heard panicked breathing. He drew his daggers and spun, searching for the source. He didn't have to search hard to find her. She was frantically sliding side-to-side before the stone wall that surrounded the teleportation spot, her hands on it, feeling it, as if her mind couldn't comprehend it was there.

Esar-Haden re-sheathed his daggers. He stepped up to her. He was right next to her yet she didn't notice him. She stared at the wall, blinking as rapidly as she was breathing. Her face was florid. Esar-Haden reached out and placed a hand on her shoulder. "Esmé." She turned her head and looked at him—eyes wide with fear. She blinked, turned to look at the wall, then turned back to him. "You've been teleported."

Esmé reached up and placed her hand over Esar-Haden's. She stood this way for some time, blinking, staring straight ahead at neither him nor the wall, but into the shadows between the pines. Esar-Haden watched her. Esmé whispered.

"Say again."

Esmé looked up at him. "My brother—you—"

Esar-Haden frowned. "You heard?"

"I—" She was cognizant of her hand on his, of their touch, of her disgust. She jerked away from him. "My brother a thief! You a—" she looked away from him, "murderer."

Esar-Haden crossed his arms.

She turned to face him. "How can my brother do this? You must have—"

"Power corrupts."

"Power corrupts?"

Esar-Haden uncrossed his arms. "I don't mean to be flippant, but, yes, it does." He stepped toward her. She didn't backpedal, as he expected. "Imagine having the power to shape reality. Imagine knowing the secret language of the gods."

She studied him with a mixture of horror and curiosity on her face.

"Once you got an ounce of that," he said, "what wouldn't you do for a pound?"

"I wouldn't—" she said, her voice breaking as she began to cry.

Esar-Haden reached out, caressed her cheek, freeing a teardrop from her soft skin. She pulled away from his touch. He looked at the bead of water on the tip of his finger. "Maybe," he looked at her, "you wouldn't be corrupted."

"Esar," she spoke in a soft tone, "you have to stop him." She reached out and took his wrist. She lowered his hand and put her own hand within, locking her fingers with his. "My brother, he isn't thinking clearly. He can't want this, not truly. This isn't our family. We weren't raised to hurt others."

Esar-Haden looked down at their hands. He looked into her face. The pleading look in her eyes, begging for a morality he lacked, made him feel dirty. He frowned, pulled his hand free, and turned away.

"Your brother said you were sheltered," he turned back, "you have what some might call a perfect life. Your innocence has been kept whole. Your mind has remained untroubled by the violence of everyday living. Despite what you might think of me, I do understand, at least to a degree, how a person like you thinks, how you perceive the world. I'm sorry to be the first to strike against your innocence but your brother is going to—"

"Kill? For a piece of paper?" asked Esmé. "Why? Life gives you everything you need to be happy." She took his hand, interlocked their fingers once more, and squeezed.

Esar-Haden frowned. "Maybe life gave *you* everything—" The look in her tear-filled eyes gave him pause. "Listen, we've got to find a hole to hide in. We're not safe here."

Esmé released his hand, stiffened her jaw, and planted her feet. "I'm going to find my brother and stop him."

"Esmé, I don't think you know your brother—"

"I know him better than you do. I'll talk him out of it."

"Once he finds out you know of his plans," said Esar-Haden, "he'll kill you."

Her features changed from defiance to shock. "He would never!"

Esar-Haden couldn't help but chuckle. "The only option now is to keep you hidden and get you back home the way you got here, teleported, with your brother ignorant of your presence. That's the only way you're staying alive."

She wanted to protest but caught herself. She realized she was talking to a dark elf, a mercenary, thief, and contract killer in the employ of her brother. If her brother had gone this far, could he be talked out of going all the way, she asked herself. She began to doubt that her brother would react in the way she assumed he would; that is, seeing the error of his way, falling to his knees with grief over the condition of his soul, and begging her and the gods for forgiveness. The danger and precariousness of her situation became clear.

Esar-Haden watched this all unfold on her face. "You'll have to live with the knowledge," he said. "But at least you'll live."

He turned and started through the pines. After a few steps he turned and offered his hand to her. "Come on." She looked at him for a long time before moving. She passed him without taking his hand.

. . .

Esar-Haden stopped her at the gate. He opened it and looked out. The town of Seven Gales was nestled in a valley beneath them. A field of alfalfa extended down the slope of the hill. Cows and horses meandered and fed. A walking path led from the hill to the town. Trees were scattered here and there but no grouping was deep enough to provide a secure place to hide.

"Let's look around," he said, trying to take her hand, but she pulled away from him—she followed him, nonetheless. He kept to the wall, circling around. He saw what he suspected was a creek lined by a thick ribbon of trees a short walk away. He headed toward it, Esmé behind him. Luckily, no farmhand spotted them.

He found a comfortable spot in the shade close to the creek and sat down. Esmé stood a few feet away. Esar-Haden searched his pockets. He pulled free a packet of smoked meat and bit off a chunk. He held it out to Esmé. She crossed her arms and turned her head.

"It's going to be a while. You might as well get comfortable." He reached into his pack and produced a wineskin, uncorked it, took a sip, then offered this to his unhappy companion.

Esmé found her obstinance a bit silly. After all, she asked herself, what else could she do but trust him. She sat down next to Esar-Haden, facing him. She took both the jerky and the wine.

"I don't often eat meat."

"I got a few pears. Want one?"

"Yes, please," she said, handing back the jerky.

Esar-Haden was digging through his pack in search of the pears when she asked, "Does that hurt?"

Esar-Haden tried to figure out what she was asking about but couldn't.

"That." She reached out and pointed at his neck.

"Oh, my tattoo." He chuckled. "It did hurt, not any more." He wiped the pear on his sleeve and handed it to her.

"What did it feel like?" She bent forward and began to trace the letters with the tip of her finger. She caught herself and pulled away. Her cheeks blushed with embarrassment.

"It felt like I was getting my throat cut."

"How did they do it?"

"Eh," he chuckled, "you don't want to know."

They sat for a while eating, taking sips from the wineskin, and listening to the fish splashing in the creek.

"Three of you?" asked Esar-Haden.

"Three of—"

"I mean, sisters. I was just thinking that I have three sisters and I wonder if he did too."

"Oh, yes, there are."

"How funny," said Esar-Haden. "We've both got three sisters but otherwise our lives couldn't be more different."

"Except you're both thieves."

He turned and looked at her, studying her expression. "Oh, yeah, that too." Again a few minutes of silence passed. "You said that your father is a wizard in the city? Judging from your family's wealth he must be a powerful man."

"Yes, I suppose he is," she sighed. "He's been in the capital most of my life. He serves the people, he says. That leaves little time for us. Oh," she added, "I know he's an important man, a good man, even, but—" Her voice fell away into silence.

Esar-Haden studied her. "I didn't know my father, either," he said, "or my mother."

She looked at him. "Who raised you?"

"No one, really. My sister, Yolandi, if you could call her abuse 'raising.' Then, the streets of Pwyll, the dark elf city I'm from."

"An orphan?"

Esar-Haden laughed. "All male dark elves are orphans of a sort. You see, in dark elf society in general, and especially in Pwyll, the males are considered inferior. This leads to all sorts of transgressions against us. Some males have it better, some worse. Anyway, I had a home to go to, a place to sleep, that is. But I spent as much time as possible in the Ghetto of White Skin, running with kids like me—throw aways."

"That's sad, Esar."

"It's been interesting, to say the least."

"My brother—" began Esmé, but stopped short. She sorted her thoughts and continued. "I think he's always felt like he could never equal our father's achievements. Even when he was a boy he drove himself relentlessly, as if trying to catch up to our father—or outrun his inner demons." She shook her head. "He never played as a child." She glanced at Esar-Haden. "He's never sang with us. He's always been—" She looked down. "And now this." She looked at him. "He frightens me. I fear what you said is true, that if I tried to stop him he would kill me." She trembled and tears fell to her cheeks. "I'm scared."

Esar-Haden scooted close to her and wrapped a comforting arm around her shoulder.

"By this time tomorrow, you'll be tending to your beautiful garden."

She looked at him. "What if you get killed?"

"Hey," he smiled and squeezed her, "that's no way to think."

"Are you really going to kill that other wizard?"

"I'm going to slip by him like a shadow. Despite what I told your bother, it's not smart to fight a wizard if you don't have to."

"What will he do with it? I mean—"

"The, what did he call it, the *Chronicle*?" Esar-Haden removed his arm from around Esmé. "Who knows? Half the time wizards think in grand schemes but then reality intercedes. He said they're mad scribbles. I bet they don't make a damn bit of sense." He smiled. "That's why I prefer gold. I know I can spend it. Never any doubt about that."

She chuckled, then sighed, then looked up at the sky through the leaves above. She looked at him, studying his face. She reached, lifted his arm, and returned it to her shoulder, leaning into him. "We've got time, you promised to recite some of your poetry."

"Yeah," he laughed. "About that."

. . .

Esar-Haden woke with a start. Esmé was still in his arms, asleep. Only a remnant of the sun's rays remained. The shade had become shadow. A chill came over Esar-Haden, causing him to shiver. He pulled the blanket from his bedroll tighter around their tangled forms.

Esmé awoke and shivered, wrapping her arms tighter around him. "Can we build a fire?"

"A little one," he said, rising. She rose too and in the semi-darkness they both dressed, both a bit shy, both a bit shocked at their quick and complete intimacy. He searched the area for fallen branches. She watched him break and assemble the branches and twigs. He stuffed dried leaves beneath them then produced a tinderbox from his pack.

"The sun's going down." She watched him light the fire and blow on the tiny flame. "I guess that means you're going to the tower?"

He looked at her. He knew that she didn't want him to go. "Stay here and keep warm," he said. "Wait maybe an hour or so, then hide in the same spot you found yourself in after being teleported. Wait there until your brother and I return. When your brother teleports us home, you sneak into your bedroom and pretend you've been there the entire time. Maybe I'll join you," he joked. She didn't laugh.

"Can you get the scroll without hurting anyone—or without getting hurt?" she asked. He didn't answer. She remained quiet for some time. The popping of sticks in the fire echoed through the trees. "What if my brother tries to kill you?"

"Why would he do that?"

"I don't know." She shook her head. "Silly thoughts. I'm just worried." She reached for him. He sat next to her and she wrapped her arms around him. "I didn't expect— I never—" She studied his face. "Don't do it. Don't go."

"I have to."

"No you don't."

"How are we going to get home without him?"

"I don't know. We'll find a way," she said. "Esar, I don't want you to get killed. In your arms I felt—"

He kissed her forehead. "I won't." He stood, breaking her hold on him. "Like a shadow, remember?" He saw that she wasn't comforted. "Esmé." She looked up at him. "I know what I'm doing." He glanced at the fire. "Keep warm. In an hour head out." He bent and cupped her chin. "In two hours I'll tuck you into bed."

. . .

Esar-Haden stood outside of the Tower of Seven Gales, gazing at what was once a thief, a second-story man, who hung from a windowsill above. He'd been turned to stone. Esar-Haden tried to see the man's face, but couldn't.

'This is where your career ended,' he thought, studying the second-story man. He worried that his might end here as well. He reached out and patted the stone thief on the rump. 'I've got an inside guy.' The thought did not mollify his fear.

He walked around the tower. When he got to the front door he stopped. A ball of blue-white light hung above the door, floating in space, attached to nothing—magical fumes held it aloft. Esar-Haden stood just at the edge of the pool of light, feet set wide, hands resting on the pommels of his daggers.

A few minutes passed. He heard movement and slid his hands down over the handles of his daggers. He turned his head so he could hear. He heard nothing more, saw nothing. A sound from the opposite direction came to him—the door latch. Esar-Haden pulled one of his daggers free. The door opened and the slender frame of the elven wizard leaned against the jam. "Well," said the elven wizard, "here we are."

Esar-Haden sheathed his dagger and stepped close to the wizard, placing his hand on the door. The wizard stepped backwards into the interior of the tower, allowing Esar-Haden to enter, then shut the door. Only the light of the moon, falling through tall windows in lazy silver arcs, illuminated the space.

Standing in an alcove that once held a bookshelf was a stone statue of a warrior. Even though it appeared as nothing more than a bit of impressive statuary, it held the promise of movement and possessed an air of menace. The elven wizard noticed Esar-Haden studying it. "The aforementioned golem. Ever see one?"

"Nope," said Esar-Haden.

"Don't worry," said the elven wizard. "Followed?"

"Not possible," said Esar-Haden. "Point me to the archives."

"Down the hall," said the elven wizard, motioning with his head. "Take the stairs down until you can go no further."

"And then?"

"And then—" The wizard grinned, turned, and started up a rough-cut stone staircase.

Esar-Haden watched him disappear into darkness. He turned and headed down the hall, daggers in-hand.

. . .

Esar-Haden stopped at the end of the hall before a partially opened door. The crackle of a torch could be heard. A stone staircase descended in a spiral. A torch burned in a holder a few feet away, throwing yellow-orange washes onto the blue-grey stone. There were torches in wall holders every ten feet, offering just enough light to annoy him. He preferred near total darkness; by which, like a cat, he could see remarkably well.

He was moving as cautiously and silently as he could. He was listening, his acute dark elf ears on alert. It was this focus that brought the sound of rustling fabric to his awareness. A second after, the light from behind him dimmed: someone or something was moving in front of the torch.

Esar-Haden turned and steadied himself on the stairs. 'Great spot for an ambush,' he cursed. 'He even has the high ground. Still, I might have the element of surprise.'

A figure came into view on the stairs. Whoever it was, they were wrapped in a dark cloak, pulled shut. The cowl was down and Esar-Haden could see nothing of the individual, except for long, strait, blood-red hair spilling out of the cowl's opening. Esar-Haden didn't want to allow the cloak to open and a wand or a raised finger sprouting lightening to emerge. He lunged upwards and thrust his main-hand dagger into the center of the cloak.

He felt no resistance. He tried to draw his hand back for a second strike but before he could the cloaked figure dissolved into black smoke. Esar-Haden thought he recognized the peculiar smell that came with the smoke, but he couldn't quite place it. The smoke curled around him, enveloped him, then spread thin until it disappeared.

'Either I met the second wizard just now or something even worse is going on.' He stood with his back against the stone wall, looking up and down the stairs, listening, waiting. Nothing came. Not a sound except for the crackling of the torches. 'No going back now,' he told himself. He took a few deep breaths and continued down the stairs.

The stairs ended in a hall. It twisted and turned for seemingly no reason other than to frustrate him. His sixth sense told him something was coming. He pressed himself into a turn in the hall and waited. He heard the click of heels on stone.

A black-stocking leg curled around the corner, ending in a mirror-polished stiletto heel. The leg slid to the ground, pulled its owner forward, into view, then disappeared into the rich, textured black cloth of a cloak.

The cloak was pulled around her, the hood up. She had her head bent, the cloth hid her face. Her blood-red hair spilled from the opening. This time Esar-Haden could detect her voluptuous curves, even under the cloak. Again the familiar smell came but again he couldn't recall where he had come across it before.

"A nice trick," he said, "the poof of smoke routine." She made no reply. She kept to the opposite side of the narrow hall, still advancing. Her stocking legs and black heels flashed in and out of the open front of the cloak. Esar-Haden leveled his off-hand dagger in front of him, defensively. He pulled the main-hand dagger down to his waist, ready to strike with it. "Going to risk it again?"

The cloaked figure did not lift her head, did not reveal herself. She was close enough for him to strike. Still, she did not slow her approach. As she passed she reached out. Her hand was gloved in black satin, extending all the way to her elbow. Esar-Haden tensed. She traced the edge of his dagger's blade with one finger. Esar-Haden swore that he heard her purr. She withdrew her hand and pulled the cloak shut. She spun, the cloak twirling and began to walk back the way she'd came. Within seconds she was around the bend, gone from view.

He hadn't expected an obstacle quite like this. He followed her. For a moment he had the suspicion he himself was being followed. He didn't hear a sound, however. He chalked it up to a growing sense of paranoia.

He kept on the trail of the voluptuous, cloaked entity. The hall had so many bends and turns he could hardly keep sight of her. He could only catch the black cloak as it disappeared around corners.

'What are you doing?' he asked himself. 'You're an idiot to follow her. You told Esmé you knew what you were doing but this is amateur stuff.' He berated himself. 'You know you're walking into a trap. Turn around, find Esmé, and get out of here!' Yet, even as he thought it, he knew he wasn't going to turn back. He was too damned curious. Besides, mysterious female or no, he had a job to do, and he was just stupid enough to persist.

The mysterious, cloaked female led him into a natural cavern. In the center of the cavern was a stone dais. Situated on this dais was a circular mattress piled high with furs. Once in the chamber, the cloaked figure turned to face him, drawing back the hood. The features of her face were perfect, too perfect.

She had red-painted lips, high cheekbones, and large dark eyes framed in smoky-red. Esar-Haden frowned when he saw the small horns protruding from her forehead. He knew a demon when he saw one. He realized the familiar smell—brimstone. He had smelled it in Maljamir, the deepest of the trio of caves that made up Pwyll—the cave inhabited by demons. Although he knew what she was, his eyes couldn't stop exploring. She knew they couldn't. She flung her cloak open so he could continue.

A leather under-bust corset thrust her breasts forward. She wore a short, black leather skirt. Her hips curved dramatically. A pair of crimson, featherless wings extended from her back.

The succubus let the cloak fall to the floor. She advanced, her heels clicking, until she stood in front of Esar-Haden. She was a foot taller than he was. She looked down at him. Her wings extended, wrapping around him, situating the pair in their own private space. Esar-Haden knew what she could do. He knew how dangerous she was. He also knew that his daggers, not being heavily enough enhanced with magic, couldn't even break her skin. He sheathed them.

"I'm looking for a scroll."

"No scrolls here." She reached out and traced a finger along his jawline, licking her blood-red lips as she did so.

"You wouldn't mind if I poked around in the corners just to be sure?" Esar-Haden reached up and pressed against her wing, hoping to find his way out of her demonic embrace.

"Do you find me attractive?" Her voice slithered into his head. He felt the compulsion to compliment her, to feed her ego, to please her—to worship her. He knew it was part of her power. He fought it. A halting, choking laughter came from somewhere outside of the winged enclosure. Esar-Haden looked into the succubus's enchanting eyes.

"Friend of yours?"

"Lover."

"Ah."

Her wings pressed against Esar-Haden's back, forcing his body against hers. He looked up. She bent her head and dragged her lips against his cheek. She kissed her way to his ear. "What's your name?" While she waited for an answer, she busied herself with biting his neck.

"Esar-Haden."

"Where did you come from, Esar-Haden?" She was kissing, biting, and sucking on the juncture where his neck met his jaw, just below his ear. He felt his temperature rising.

"Pwyll."

She pulled back and looked at him, recognition in her eyes.

"Heard of it?"

"Maljamir?" she asked. Esar-Haden nodded. Her shapely lips turned into a frown. "You're one of the Sidonai?"

"That's right," said Esar-Haden.

"You're a long way from home, Sidonai." She narrowed her eyes. "A long way from your masters."

"Perhaps," said Esar-Haden, his smile turning into a firm line. The succubus retracted her wings. Esar-Haden became aware of a short, twisted body next to his. He glanced over at the man. Her "lover" stood no more than five feet tall, due to painful-looking contortions of his bones and musculature. The man's head was bulbous; the features of his face were shoved to one side. A second face, infantile and placid, was scrunched next to the first. Esar-Haden shuddered and looked back to the much more pleasing body of the succubus.

The succubus turned and walked a few steps toward the dais before stopping. She looked over her shoulder at Esar-Haden, saw his eyes on her, and smiled. She arced her back and thrust out her hips.

"Lover," she said, her voice like silk. "Make the Sidonai *comfortable*."

"Yes, Mistress," said the jumbled, distorted, two-faced man. He crooked an arm and extended a finger. Esar-Haden went for a dagger but was too late. A black arc of energy shot from the man's gnarled finger. Esar-Haden screamed in pain and fell unconscious to the ground.

. . .

The smell of brimstone once again filled Esar-Haden's nostrils. He opened his eyes. He was lying on the rough stone of the cave floor, on his side. His hands were bound behind his back. His ankles were tied together. He could see that his belt and daggers were lying on the dais. The succubus was reclining on the furs, her dark eyes on him. She held a whip in her hand. It snaked down, traveling across her legs, curling up next to her black stiletto heels.

A second scent caught his attention. He recognized it. "Esmé!?" He looked around. She stumbled into view. "What—"

One of her eyes was starting to swell shut, her skin discolored from bruising, and there was fresh blood on her lips. She stopped, looked at him, then lunged forward, having been pushed. Her brother came into view, laughing. Esmé tried to rush forward, toward Esar-Haden, but her brother was quicker. He reached out and grabbed a fistful of hair, halting her.

"You—" yelled Esar-Haden. "What's she doing here?"

"She—" began the elven wizard.

"We're here for the scroll," interrupted Esar-Haden. "What's this—"

"Oh, Esar-Haden, how obtuse."

"Silence!" commanded the succubus, her voice rebounded around the cave. "These two are suitable for the ritual?"

"Yes, Mistress," answered the elven wizard. "A dark elf thief and murderer. Something evil and corrupt, as the ritual calls for and—" Esar-Haden could see the smile widening on his face. "An innocent, a virgin, something pure." He laughed. "My own sister."

"You bastard!" interjected Esar-Haden.

"You did exactly as I expected, sister," said the elven wizard, ignoring the dark elf's condemnation. "You took the bait—the ebony-skinned worm." He laughed, glancing at Esar-Haden. "When you felt the hook you panicked. Now you'll—"

"Brother! Please!" pleaded Esmé.

"Ugh. Enough of your whining," said the elven wizard. He shoved her down. She fell into a heap on the floor. "Stay!" he commanded. He approached the dais. "Mistress, may I?"

The succubus nodded. The elven wizard crawled on top of the furs, making his way to her. He curled up beside her and looked at the two fools he'd lured to their end, a smug, satisfied look on his face. "Have I done well, Mistress? Are you happy?"

"You brought me your own sister? A nice touch." He looked up into her face, just in time to see her smile turned to a frown. "There's just one problem." She pointed at Esar-Haden. "He's a Sidonai." The elven wizard looked confused.

"A Sidonai? I've never heard of—"

"He's spoken for," she said, "his soul—claimed by the fiends of Maljamir."

Esar-Haden watched the color drain from the elven wizard. He looked from Esar-Haden to the succubus. "I—"

"However," she interrupted. "A claim is only a claim. I possess him now and that's all that matters." At hearing this the elven wizard visibly relaxed.

"Are you sure about that?" asked Esar-Haden. "You don't want to piss off the wrong demonic lord."

The succubus shot him an angry glance. "It's too late for you." She looked to the two-faced man. "Seruli, draw the circle." She nudged the elven wizard. He guessed her will and slid from the dais.

He walked over to Esar-Haden, crouching next to him. "You said you were the best. Ha! Look at you." He reached out and moved Esar-Haden's white hair out of his face. "Did you like my little ruse? I worked hard on it. Like writing a fiction, you have to get every detail right. When Oltropp suggested—"

"Your own sister?" asked Esar-Haden.

The elf looked to the sobbing, pathetic form of his sister. "Demonic rituals are complicated, Esar-Haden. Any old human sacrifice won't do. The ritual we are going to perform today has *detailed* requirements."

"Listen to me," whispered Esar-Haden. "I know you're an arrogant prick, you think you can control everything. You're as smart as they come, aren't you?" The elven wizard smiled in response. Esar-Haden continued. "A succubus? A demonic ritual? You have no idea what you're getting yourself into. Believe me, I know."

The elven wizard seemed to be contemplating the dark elf's words. He leaned in close to Esar Haden, "What's a Sidonai?"

"You think you're going to give me and your sister over to some demon and reap the rewards? It doesn't work that way. I'm not the price, I'm the bait, *you* pay the price."

"We'll see, Esar. Now, you'll have to excuse me. I should help Seruli, he has bad eyesight." With that the wizard rose and walked over to the hunched figure of the deformed man.

Esar-Haden turned to Esmé. "Psst," he whispered. She lifted her tear-streaked face from her hands and looked over to him. "Get out of here!" She blinked several times with her un-swollen eye, staring at him, not comprehending. "Esmé! You aren't tied up. Get the hell out of here."

"She's not going anywhere," said the succubus. "The poor thing is in shock. This is all too much for her fragile mind. Be quiet!" The succubus turned away from her captives and kept an eye on her lovers.

Esar-Haden watched as the circle was drawn. The deformed wizard held a copper pot in the crook of his left arm. He dipped his fingers into it and drew them out covered in blood. He bent awkwardly and sketched out the circle and magic runes on the floor, mumbling the necessary words as he did so. The elven wizard stood close to him, repeating the words.

When the circle was completed Seruli crossed the room raised his fingers to the flame of a torch. The blood on his fingers ignited, burning a blue-green. He shuffled back to the circle, bent once more, and lit the blood on the floor. The fire consumed the blood, leaving behind a sticky black residue.

"Excellent!" said the succubus. She looked to Esar-Haden and Esmé.

The two wizards approached.

"Esmé! Run!" Esar-Haden yelled, as he tried to scoot away from them. He didn't get far. Seruli grabbed his ankle and with a grunt began to drag him across the room. Esar tried to wiggle and fight, but there was little he could do. The elven wizard grabbed his own sister by the hair. He took visible relish in dragging her into the infernal diagram. Then both of them left the circle.

"Esmé," whispered Esar-Haden. "Untie me! Esmé, come on, girl, snap out of it." Esmé was slumped next to him, her eyes shut, her lithe frame shaken by her crying. "Esmé, please—"

The succubus laughed. "Look at the fierce dark elf killer beg a frightened child for help. You delight me, Esar-Haden."

"Esar?" whispered Esmé. Esar-Haden glanced toward the dais. Both Seruli and Esmé's brother were standing before the succubus, awaiting orders.

"Untie my wrists. Hurry."

"What's happening?" moaned Esmé. "Are we going to die?"

The succubus bent forward and grabbed Esar-Haden's belt. She stood and crossed the short distance between the dais and the ritual circle. Both of her lovers followed her. She crouched, hovering over both Esmé and Esar. "The Sidonai certainly are fearless," she mused. "Must be the few drops of demonic blood you've got swirling around in you." She rose, drew out one of Esar-Haden's daggers, and handed it to the elven wizard. "A souvenir." She flipped her hair and uncurled her wings. She tossed the belt and second dagger into the darkness at the edge of the cave. "Begin the ritual."

The wizards and the succubus took up their positions and began to chant.

Esar-Haden rolled over onto his other side so he could better communicate with Esmé.

"This thing's going to go horribly wrong," he whispered. "When it does—"

Before he could finish the hairs on his neck rose. The air became charged. A black ball, crawling with electricity, formed in the air above Esmé and him. The voices of the trio were soon lost in the crackling of energy. The ball expanded, first, slowly, then, in one frightening swell. The ball exploded in silence, filling the room with an inky darkness.

A slender figure could be seen. She hovered at the center of the magic circle, above and just to the side of Esar and Esmé. She was not only slender but small. It took a moment for Esar-Haden to realize it was a trick of perspective. She was far away, still locked in the Abyss, struggling to cross over. From what Esar-Haden could make out the demon was ebony-skinned, like him. Unlike him, she was wreathed in flames of scintillating, shifting colors.

The succubus saw her as well. "Syrryx, the Light in the Darkness," she said, her voice reverent. "She comes!"

The form of Syrryx grew larger and larger. The ritual was working. She was crossing over. Visibly, she still appeared to be a significant distance away, but her power projected forward, onto this plane.

"Yes." He heard her say. Her voice a whisper at his ear, a whisper devoid of the wet heat that belonged to it. "Your soul has black marks. Every life you've taken has left an indelible stain. You will be the salt, the bitter taste to offset the sweet. I will devour you last, to remind me of the sorrow of life."

Esar-Haden felt her touch leave him. The echo of her voice remained at his ear a moment longer. "I will devour her," there was a pause, "first. I will savor her innocence. She is the sweetness, purity, the absence of sin. The delicate flower of life."

Esar-Haden was looking into Esmé's face when the color drained from it. The cold touch was on her now. A scream filled the room, but not from Esmé. It was a scream that traveled across a great expanse of space. A scream that was so anguished it pained the occupants of the room to hear it.

The room was instantly filled with the angry hissing and crackling of electricity. It came from the darkness at the edges of the room and drove its way into the miniature form of Syrryx. She screamed in pain. It was the angry magic of a ritual gone wrong.

"No!" cried the succubus. "What's happening?" She looked back and forth between her lovers. "What's happening?"

The answer came from Syrryx, who screamed through the pain. "Impure!" A bolt of electricity silenced her. The distant demon hung in the air between worlds, held aloft on arcs of thick, white lightning. The succubus stood in shocked silence. She looked back and forth between Esar-Haden and Esmé. "What?" she asked, her voice barely audible above the popping and buzz of the electricity. She turned to the elven wizard. "You said—" But her words were stolen from her as the electricity curled downwards and reached between her breasts.

"Agh!" The elven wizard was struck rigid by a bolt of electricity. The single bolt was followed by several others, angry magic lashing out at its authors. Esar-Haden rolled over onto his other side. He searched for Seruli. He soon found the grotesque form of the wizard. He had been knocked to the floor, bolts of electricity pressing him down. Seruli's body convulsed, but it was clear he was dead.

Esar-Haden turned back over. He was about to speak when the electricity found its way to him. The first shock took his breath away. The second set his skin on fire, or so it felt. The magic leapt from him to Esmé. He watched, helplessly, as the electricity drove into her. Her muscles spasmed. She flopped and twisted. The electricity danced along her body, causing her to twirl over onto her other side. The flashing energy went elsewhere. Esar-Haden saw something white-hot glowing at her back. Something tucked into her belt.

Now the electricity converged on the demon mother, the Light in the Darkness. It blotted out the fire she wreathed herself in with its own angry color.

Esmé moved. She groped, touching herself, identifying the pain. Esar-Haden, disciplined by the harsh tortures of his youth, could control his reaction to pain. Still, it took him several seconds to find his voice.

"Esmé."

She moaned, but not in response to him. She was still lost in her pain. In the background Esar-Haden could hear the screaming of Syrryx. The sound was growing more and more distant, like a wounded animal howling as it ran away from its attacker.

Esar-Haden tried to scan the room but the blinding white column of energy was right above him. He closed his eyes. The pillar of light remained as an after image. The lighting moved and he opened his eyes.

"The garden shears! Esmé!" He was screaming over the deafening roar of electricity. Then, as quickly as the electricity had turned on them, it was gone. Silence fell over the room. The ritual had failed. The requirements had not been met. Esmé was no virgin.

Esar-Haden opened his eyes. The ghostly after image was slow to fade but he was still able to map the room. Seruli was dead, heaped in a corner, his body smoldering. The elven wizard was alive, on all fours, his head down, trying to vomit but unable to. The succubus had been driven back to the cave's wall. She was half collapsed against the blasted stone, but still somehow kept her feet under her. Her once perfect skin was criss-crossed with raised black wounds which seeped black blood. She absent-mindedly touched her lower abdomen, in the gap between her corset and her skirt. A deep gash revealed the tender meat within. Esar-Haden returned his gaze to Esmé.

"Esmé. I need you."

Esmé registered his voice. She halted her efforts to calm the pain and turned her head a degree. She offered her profile to him but she was not entire conscious of her actions. She was in a daze.

"The shears," he said. "Your gardening shears."

She turned her head still further. She twisted her torso. "Esar?"

"Esmé—the shears! You must have tucked them into your belt. Do you remember? Cut me free."

Esmé reached down and grabbed the shears. The tang of burnt flesh filled the air. She rolled over, now facing Esar-Haden.

Esar-Haden turned onto his side. He twisted his neck, looking over his shoulder at Esmé. "Cut the rope."

Esmé cut the rope. Esar-Haden worked his hands free. He took the shears from her, they were cooling but still painful to hold. He reached down, and cut his feet free of their bindings.

"Finally," he cursed, tossing the shears aside.

Esar-Haden got to his feet, crouching next to Esmé. "Can you walk?"

She only moaned in response.

Esar-Haden scanned the cave. "There you are." He left Esmé's side and rushed over his belt. The sole remaining dagger had fallen out of its sheath. He picked up his belt, scooped up his dagger, and dropped it into one of the empty sheaths. He returned to Esmé and thrust an arm under hers. He began to lift her up. "Come on."

Despite all she had endured Esmé found her feet. She clung to him. Esar-Haden half carried her, half pushed her toward the hall. As he approached the exit of the cave a figure stumbled into view. It was Esmé's brother. He held a slender wand in his hand. His other arm hung limp at his side. The elven wizard started to speak, perhaps to activate the wand, perhaps to threaten Esar-Haden, either way, he never got the words out.

Esar-Haden flung Esmé forward. She collided into her brother, knocking the wand wide. Her brother twisted his body, causing her to ricochet off of him. She collapsed in a heap next to him with a pained yelp. The elven wizard looked to Esar-Haden. He was surprised to see the dark elf was face-to-face with him. He started to bring the wand up, but it was too late.

He became aware of a sharp pain in his abdomen. He glanced down and saw a dagger buried in his stomach. The wand slipped from his fingers. Esar-Haden let go of the dagger's handle and stepped back. The wizard fingered the pommel. Esar-Haden reached forward and withdrew his second dagger from the elven wizard's belt. "No souvenir for you," he said, as he replaced the blade in its sheath. The elven wizard started to stumble backwards but Esar reached out and steadied him.

The elven wizard searched the room, tilting his head to see past Esar-Haden.

"There," said Esar-Haden, leaning to the side so that the elven wizard could see the succubus. She sat against the wall, her stocking legs sticking straight out. A pool of black blood radiated out from her.

"She's dying," observed Esar-Haden.

The elven wizard looked into his face. The news seemed to shock him.

"I tried to warn you," said Esar-Haden. Esmé staggered to her feet. "Sorry about that, darling. I had to think fast." She was studying her brother's back. A look of realization then horror crossed her face. Esar-Haden frowned. He knocked the elf's hand away and took ahold of the dagger's hilt. He slid the knife out. In his periphery he saw Esmé flutter to the floor like a leaf.

"My Mistress is—dying?" The elven wizard reached out and grabbed Esar-Haden's arm to steady himself. His legs were growing weak.

"You're dying."

The elven wizard once again looked at him with a shocked expression. The color drained from his face and he wobbled. He reached out with his other hand, somehow getting his injured arm to respond. Esar-Haden offered his other arm and the wizard took it.

A trickle of blood found its way between his lips and dribbled from his chin. "When did you?"

"You left us together all day."

"I never—"

"The seduction route—" began Esar-Haden.

"But—"

"I told you it was double-edged."

The elven wizard glanced down at Esmé then looked back at Esar-Haden. "It was a cute plan."

"You should have been a dark elf," said Esar-Haden.

"Maybe our souls will meet in the Abyss—cousin."

Esar-Haden shrugged his shoulders. The stomach wound sapped the wizard's remaining strength. He collapsed into a seated position. Esar-Haden knelt down with him. The wizard slid his hand down until it grasped Esar-Haden's. He studied his own pale skin as it contrasted against the ebony skin of his distant, darkness-dwelling cousin. He looked into Esar-Haden's eyes.

Esar-Haden watched as the elf's eyes glazed over. He lost his grip and settled down into dying. Esar-Haden stood and went to Esmé. He knelt and picked her up. He flung her over his left shoulder, keeping his right hand free incase he needed the dagger, not that he felt he would survive yet another "obstacle." He started out of the cave.

"Esar?"

Esar-Haden stopped and half turned, looking down at the slouched wizard. The dying elf began to cough. A line of blood and saliva hung from his mouth.

"You have a long walk home." He turned his head and looked up into Esar-Haden's eyes. "Sorry about that."

Esar-Haden turned and looked over his shoulder at the succubus. She was slumped forward, enduring her last moments of life. The elf looked to her as well. Esar-Haden looked down at Esmé's brother. "It will take some time to bleed out. You've got time to think." He turned and took a step into the hallway, then stopped, turning back. "Sorry about that."

H. Rad Bethlen has been compared to Isak Dinesen (*Seven Gothic Tales*) and Fritz Leiber (*Swords and Deviltry*). He is known for his work in the fantasy and horror genres as well as his non-fiction. He has been published in Europe and America.

Enjoy the story?

If you liked what you read, please take a moment to **leave a review on Amazon**! Your feedback helps other readers find this story. It only takes a minute but it makes a huge difference. The Amazon algorithm requires 30-50 reviews before it will pick this book up and promote it to like-minded readers. Your review is instrumental in helping that happen!

For more great fiction and non-fiction please visit:

roosterandravenpublishing.com

hradbethlen.com

or H. Rad Bethlen's Amazon page.

www.ingramcontent.com/pod-product-compliance
Lightning Source LLC
Chambersburg PA
CBHW071223130626
46555CB00004B/1816